We Stand Together, Just

(A book to explain Coronavirus to kids)

Written by: Dr. Renee Kleris, Dr. Katherine Clarridge & Dr. Rebecca MacDonell-Yilmaz

Illustrated by: Catherine Wilson

There once was a time when we could roam far from home, whenever and wherever we wanted.

But a virus came around,
spread through cities and towns,
and life as we knew it halted.

You may ask, "What's the issue?"
Let me get you a tissue.
Coronavirus made people sick.

It wasn't picky and made people feel icky,
Whether their names were George, Mia, or Nick.

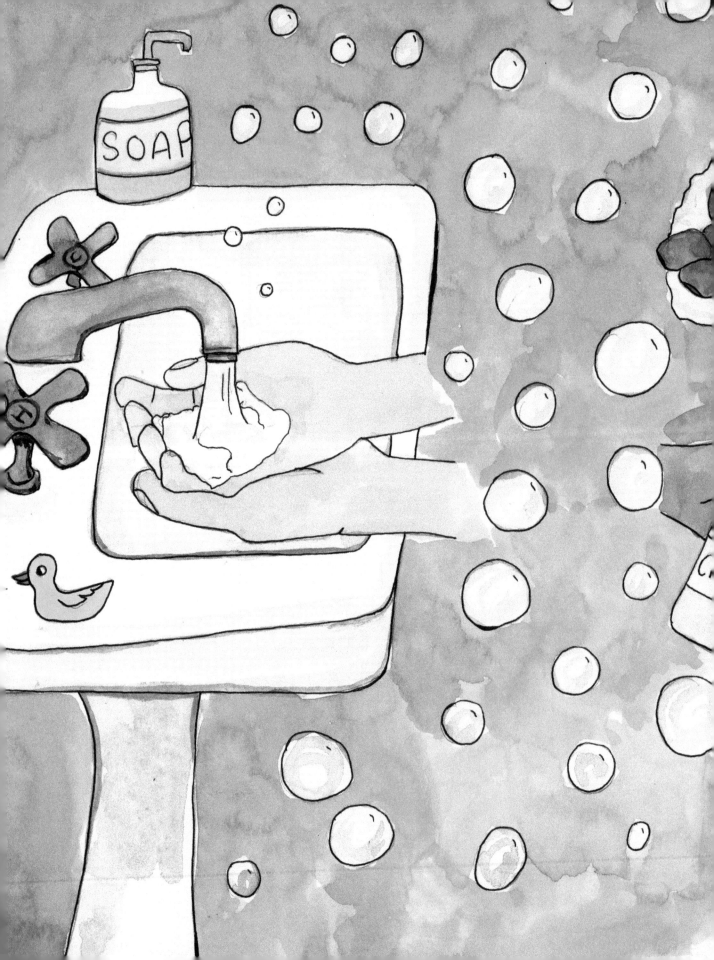

It traveled in the air from here to there
through coughs and sneezes - ACHOO!
There was no cure, but to keep our hands pure,
Staying home was the best thing to do.

Grocers and drivers worked late to fill every plate,
and cleaners kept each surface pristine.

Doctors and nurses cared for the sick,
while scientists hurried to make a vaccine.

Parks and playgrounds shut down in every town.
School lessons were all taught from afar,

We held parties by phone to feel less alone,
and waved through the windows of cars.

Now, you might feel lazy or even stir-crazy,
but this virus is very contagious.

Just look around, love still abounds
and we must try to be courageous.

It will take many days, but phase by phase
life will feel more like it used to.
Going to stores, spending more time outdoors,
You'll have choices and fun things to do.

So when you feel weary, or the days get dreary
do your best to take heart.

Always remember, we're in this together,
even when we're six feet apart.

CPSIA information can be obtained
at www.ICGtesting.com
Printed in the USA
BVHW021718160221
600262BV00018B/1053